7000071624

D0536618

UWE
University
BRIS

EDUCATION
RESOURCES

To The Very Kind
John, Mary and Miriam Kiki
J.D.

For Rowan,
My Very Big
D.G.

Y
Being lost
CF

TRANSWORLD PUBLISHERS
a division of The Random House Group Ltd
61-63 Uxbridge Road, London W5 5SA

RANDOM HOUSE AUSTRALIA PTY LTD
20 Alfred St, Milsons Point, NSW 2061

RANDOM HOUSE NEW ZEALAND
18 Poland Road, Glenfield, Auckland 10

RANDOM HOUSE (PTY) LTD
Endulini, 5A Jubilee Road,
Parktown 2193, South Africa

Published in 2000 by Doubleday
a division of Transworld Publishers

Text copyright © Joyce Dunbar 2000
Illustrations copyright © Debi Gliori 2000
Designed by Ian Butterworth

The right of Joyce Dunbar to be identified as the Author
and of Debi Gliori as the illustrator of this work
has been asserted in accordance with
the Copyright, Designs and Patents Act l988

A catalogue record for this book is available
from the British Library

ISBN 0 385 60000 3

All rights reserved. No part of this publication may
be reproduced, stored in a retrieval system, or
transmitted in any form or by any means,
electronic, mechanical, photocopying, recording,
or otherwise, without the prior permission of
the publishers

Printed in Singapore

UWE, BRISTOL LIBRARY SERVICES

The
Very
Small

Joyce Dunbar

Illustrated by

Debi Gliori

DOUBLEDAY

LONDON · NEW YORK · TORONTO · SYDNEY · AUCKLAND

One day, when Giant Baby Bear
was playing in the woods, he found a very small...

...something!

He picked up the very small something
in his paws and gave it a good sniff.
"You're very small," said Giant Baby Bear.
"I'm lost," cried The Very Small. "I want my mummy!"

"I don't know where your mummy is,"
said Giant Baby Bear,
"but you can share my mummy if you like."
And he took The Very Small home to his mother
and placed it in one of her very large paws.
His mother gave a great big grin
showing all her great big teeth.
"What's this you've found?"
said Giant Mummy Bear.

"I want my daddy!" howled The Very Small.

"I don't know where your daddy is,"
said Giant Baby Bear,
"but you can share my daddy if you like."
And Giant Baby Bear took The Very Small from his
mummy's very large paws and placed him in
his daddy's even larger paws.
Giant Daddy Bear stared hard through his spectacles.
"What's this you've found?" he growled.

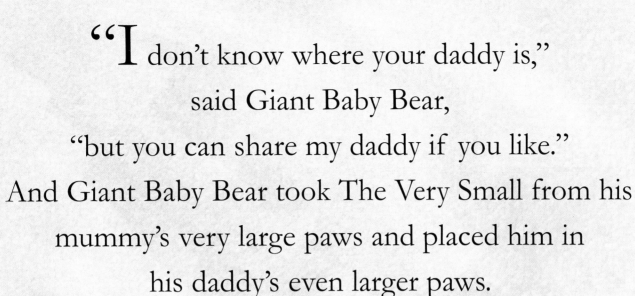

"I want to go home," wailed The Very Small.

"I don't know where your home is," said Giant Baby Bear, "but you can share my home if you like. Let me show you around."

And Giant Baby Bear showed The Very Small all around his cave. He showed him the sleeping corner and the eating corner and the scratching corner and the thinking corner. And last of all he showed him his toys in the playing corner. "There you are," said Giant Baby Bear. "You are so very small that I shall make a very small playground for you to play in."

And The Very Small rode on the very small see-saw
with Giant Baby Bear pressing one end with his paw.
And he swung on the very small swing with
Giant Baby Bear pushing.

And he slid on the very small slide with Giant Baby Bear catching him in his paws.

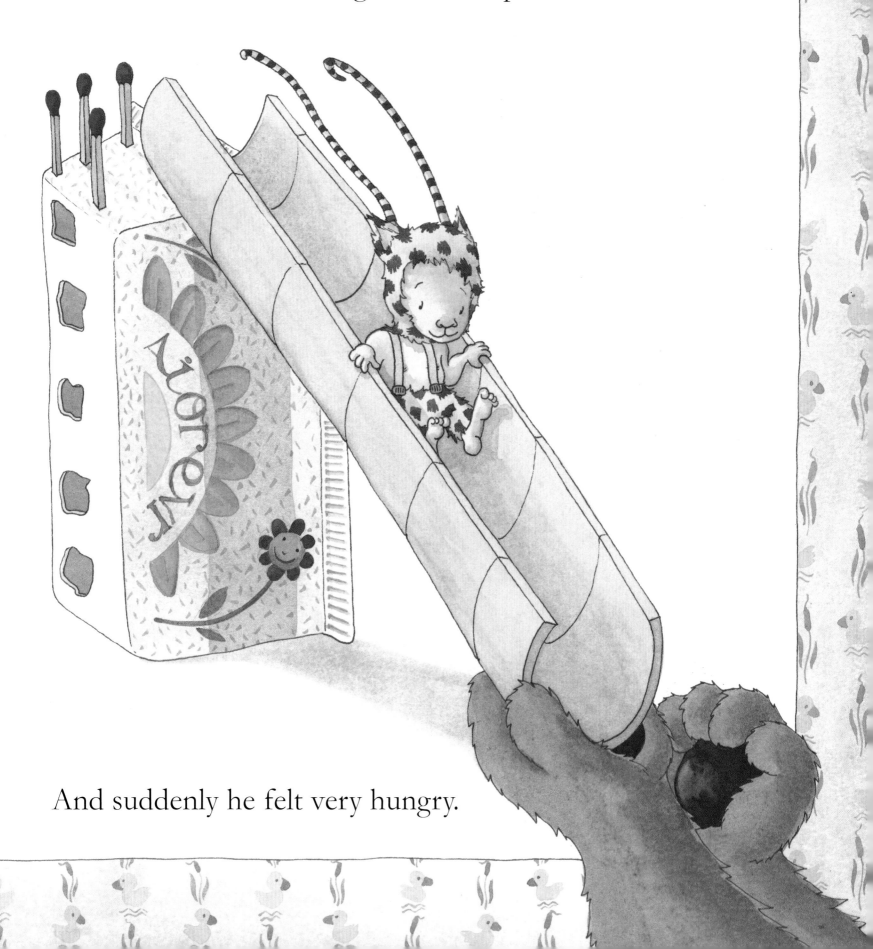

And suddenly he felt very hungry.

"I want my dinner!" called The Very Small.

"I don't know what you were going to have for your dinner," said Giant Baby Bear,

"but you can share my dinner if you like."

And Giant Baby Bear placed The Very Small next to his plate, and The Very Small ate one whole pea and five whole crumbs of bread and he drank a whole spoonful of milk.

And then he felt very tired.

"I want my bed," said The Very Small.

"I want my bed too," said Giant Baby Bear,

"but first of all we have a bath."

And Giant Baby Bear had a splashing bath

in a great big tub, while The Very Small had

a floating bath in the soapdish.

Then Giant Baby Bear put The Very Small
right next to him on his pillow and fell asleep.
But The Very Small didn't fall asleep. Giant Baby Bear
was snoring so loudly that he couldn't.
So he pinched Giant Baby Bear's nose to try to
stop him snoring, but to Giant Baby Bear it felt very much
like a tickle and suddenly he went

...blowing The Very Small right out of the cave and across the yard and over the

treetops until he landed in the very same part of the woods where he had got lost in the first place!

And there, waiting for him, were The Very Small's very own mummy and daddy. They were so pleased to see him. They took him home and tucked him up in his very own bed with his very own bear who suddenly seemed...

Very Small!